HAUNTED

This is a work of fiction. All of the characters, events, and organizations portrayed in this work are either products of the authors' imagination or used fictitiously.

Haunted: The Great Lakes Ghost Project

For information about production rights, visit:
www.jzettelmaier.com

Published by Sordelet Ink
WWW.SORDELETINK.COM

Cover by David Blixt

HAUNTED

THE GREAT LAKES GHOST PROJECT

A DEVISED PLAY BY

JOSEPH ZETTELMAIER

SORDELET
ink

HAUNTED: THE GREAT LAKES GHOST PROJECT
premiered on October 4th, 2019 at Roustabout Theatre
Troupe, Ypsilanti, MI. It was directed by Anna Simmons.
Set and Prop Design by Jennifer Maiseloff. Lighting Design
by Alex Gay. Costume Design by Josie Lapczynski. Sound
and Projection Design by Will Myers. Stage Managed by
Rebecca Goodwin. The cast was as follows:

Actor 1: Dan Johnson
Actor 2: Alysia Kolascz
Actor 3: Julia Garlotte
Actor 4: Allison Megroet

Playwright's note: HAUNTED was created using
testimonials as part of the Great Lakes Ghost Project.
The playwright retains ownership of all submitted
stories.

For information about production rights,
visit www.jzettelmaier.com.

Cast of Characters

ONE
Author

TWO
Student 1, Em, Old Woman, Caretaker, Melody

THREE
Student 2, Des, Carol, Meg, Mom

FOUR
David Payne, Col, Roommate, Sue, Female Ghost

Time
The Present, and other times

Place
Various

HAUNTED

(Lights rise. The space is representational of many times, many places, but all should seem eerie, run down, haunting. Four people enter, dressed in modern clothes. They speak to the audience)

ONE
I dwell in a lonely house I know
That vanished many a summer ago,
And left no trace but the cellar walls,
And a cellar in which the daylight falls
And the purple-stemmed wild raspberries grow.

TWO
O'er ruined fences the grape-vines shield
The woods come back to the mowing field;
The orchard tree has grown one copse
Of new wood and old where the woodpecker chops;
The footpath down to the well is healed.

THREE
I dwell with a strangely aching heart
In that vanished abode there far apart

On that disused and forgotten road
That has no dust-bath now for the toad.
Night comes; the black bats tumble and dart;

FOUR
The whippoorwill is coming to shout
And hush and cluck and flutter about:
I hear him begin far enough away
Full many a time to say his say
Before he arrives to say it out.

THREE
It is under the small, dim, summer star.
I know not who these mute folk are
Who share the unlit place with me—
Those stones out under the low-limbed tree
Doubtless bear names that the mosses mar.

TWO
They are tireless folk, but slow and sad—
Though two, close-keeping, are lass and lad—
With none among them that ever sings,
And yet, in view of how many things,
As sweet companions as might be had.

ONE
Ghost House, by Robert Frost. It's a favorite of mine.

TWO
Maybe you know this, maybe you don't...

THREE
But the incomparable Mr. Frost lived in Michigan for
six years.

FOUR
A professor at U of M.

ONE
The vanished abode, the disused and forgotten road...
the strangely aching heart. That's the part that just kills
me. I know that ache. I've felt it. The place in your
memory that you'll never see again. It stays with you...
it haunts you.

TWO
That's what it means to be haunted. Something that
stays with you, follows you...

THREE
...possesses you...

FOUR
...whether you want it to or not. It stays with you.

(Beat)

TWO
I was eighteen when I saw it.

FOUR
I was twelve...

THREE
Ten...

ONE
...twenty-five when I saw it.

TWO
Just a girl.

FOUR
No bigger than this.

(FOUR indicates a short height)

ONE
I'd been out of college for a few years.

THREE
It was something my grampa told me.

FOUR
You know how it is. A bunch of kids around a camp-fire...

ONE
Maybe there's some beers.

TWO
There were definitely beers.

THREE
People tell stories. It's what you do.

FOUR
I mean, it was October after all.

THREE
There's a fire, you roast marshmallows, you tell stories.

TWO
And drink beers.

ONE
Oh my god. I had one. ONE.

THREE
Other times, you're alone.

FOUR
But you're not alone.

TWO
You can't see anyone, can't hear anyone.

FOUR
But you know it all the same. Someone...

ONE
SomeTHING.

FOUR
...is there. With you. Watching you.

TWO
It can be the littlest thing.

ONE
A book falls off a shelf. One book. None of the others budge an inch.

TWO
Or a painting...one that feels...inhabited. Like it's watching you. Curious. Or angry.

ONE
It can be much bigger, of course.

FOUR
You're asleep and you hear...something.

TWO
Footsteps when you're all alone.

THREE
Breathing right next to your ear.

FOUR
And if it speaks...no. No freaking way. I'm out.

ONE
We love them. We fear them. We collect them and share them. All the way back to Ichabod Crane and a little town called Sleepy Hollow.

THREE
Ghost stories. The kind that get passed down.

FOUR
Not passed away.

TWO
The kind that go on and on.

ONE
Not always. Some belong just to those who saw them.

THREE
But more get told. It eases the burden.

FOUR
Makes you feel less...

ONE
Alone.

(The scene changes as ONE becomes the AUTHOR)

AUTHOR
In the summer of 2017, I started a project. For two months, I'd collect ghost stories, specifically ghost stories that happened in the Midwest. Even more specifically, stories that happened in the Great Lakes states.

TWO
Why?

AUTHOR
Why the Midwest? Or why do it at all?

THREE
The first, then the second.

(The other three walk off as the AUTHOR speaks)

AUTHOR
Fair. Why the Great Lakes? I was born in Michigan... Ann Arbor, specifically. Maize and Blue all the way. I've lived several other places, but I kept coming back here.

And then one day, I stopped moving. Home is home, and when you find that place, it stays with you, I suppose.

(Beat. AUTHOR smiles, almost mutters to himself)

AUTHOR
...the things that stay with you...

(Beat)

AUTHOR
So...yes, I wanted these stories to reflect this part of America...its history, its nature, its...eeriness, I guess. That abandoned house you've driven by a hundred times that gives you the creeps. The wide cornfield with that one scarecrow that just seems...I wanted to share what I love about this state, through the lens of its ghosts. Why do the project at all?

(Beat)

AUTHOR
It's easy to think that the internet age has made the world immortal, that all history has been recorded and categorized and made accessible. It's easy to think that, but it isn't true. Our stories still belong to us, and for many people, they're not shared unless you ask them to be. I wanted to open that invitation, to hear personal stories that can't be found by a well-worded Google search.

(An old window is projected on the upstage screen. The AUTHOR doesn't see it, but knows it's there)

AUTHOR
I've always felt that people either believe in ghosts, or they wish they did. Me? I...I don't believe. Not fully. But Christ, what I'd give to believe. I'm that person that goes to a haunted house or historical battle site and

I'm ready to go. Just give me something, ANYTHING, I can see with my own two eyes and I'm there! But so far, I've...

(The window glows. The AUTHOR works hard not to look)

AUTHOR
It's not simple. Belief. It's maybe the hardest thing in the world, even when every fiber of you wants to feel it. I've always thought of myself as an imaginative rationalist. I absolutely think that there might be UFOs or lake monsters or Bigfoots...Bigfeet?...let's say, Bigfoots. But I have to see it, right in front of me, in a way that eliminates all doubt.

(The window glows more. A low, animalistic breathing is heard)

AUTHOR
STOP!

(The window and growl/breathing disappear. The AUTHOR takes a moment to collect himself)

AUTHOR
I was twenty-five when I saw it. Only twenty-five. But things stay with you.

(The AUTHOR goes to a desk, holding many papers. A projection of an eerie forest or ruined mine in the UP appears)

AUTHOR
For two months in the summer of 2017, many people sent me many stories. Interesting note: of all the submissions I received, only one was from a man. Every other story was from a woman. Are women more aware of the supernatural around us? I just thought it was interesting.

I also traveled to several places, especially in the Upper Peninsula. I should note that a disproportionately large number of the submissions came from the UP. I'm led to believe that the vast majority of the Midwest's ghosts actually live north of the bridge. Well, maybe not "live" but...you get what I mean.

(A projection of the interior of a very old theatre)

AUTHOR
Once I'd gotten the submissions, I spent untold hours trying to figure out how to make these things into a play. I decided to start at the beginning...the first submission really lent itself to that. Why? Because it took place in a theatre.

(The actors begin to set up a representation of a dressing room and small stage)

THREE
This theatre?

AUTHOR
No this one. The Mill Theatre at Elmhurst College is haunted. This is basically an accepted fact at this point. The number of documented paranormal events, let alone stories, that have come from this old, OLD building would certainly indicate something wicked that way came.

(A series of images of the old Mill Theatre at Elmhurst College)

AUTHOR
Built in the early 1900s in Elmhurst, Illinois, the theatre began its life as a lumberyard and paper mill that...

FOUR
Do they need to know this?

AUTHOR
Yes, they need to know this! I'm setting the environment!

FOUR
I'm just saying…

(FOUR motions to the projections)

AUTHOR
Trust me, this matters.

(FOUR relents, goes back to work. As AUTHOR describes scenes, the others perform a stylized pantomime based on the AUTHOR's descriptions)

AUTHOR
The mill and the land itself were sold to Elmhurst College in 1967. But before you assume that the ghosts involved were grizzly factory accidents, it turns out there were no recorded deaths at the mill during its many years of operation.

TWO
Not a one?

AUTHOR
Nope.

THREE
No one fell into the saws or was crushed under logs or anything?

AUTHOR
Look, I was as disappointed as you are, ok?

(Projection: The interior of the Mill Theatre)

AUTHOR
That being said, hauntings have been reported there.

More than a few. This shouldn't be surprising at all, as Elmhurst is one creepy little burgh. Their historic Crane Fischer House was once a sanitarium complete with electroshock treatments. And there's a freaking mausoleum dead in the center of town!

FOUR
Heh. Dead center.

(AUTHOR stares at FOUR)

AUTHOR
So the question I came to was, "If the Mill Theatre is haunted, as many students claim, just who is haunting it?"

(He tosses a cap to FOUR, who dons it)

AUTHOR
Thanks to research and ghost hunters, we may have an answer. In 1967, Elmhurst's theatre department welcomed a new teacher...a young man named David Payne. He was their new technical director, and they say loved by many. He was also said to have an...impish sense of humor. He was always humming as he built their sets, but silenced any student who whistled while they worked.

DAVID
It's bad luck! See, back in the day, they'd whistle to tell the stagehands when to drop sandbags! So if you whistled the wrong thing at the wrong time...BAM! Flat as a pancake!

AUTHOR
1969. The students had just returned from winter break, and they were getting ready to start building The Marriage of Figaro.

TWO
Classic.

(TWO & THREE become STUDENTS 1 & 2. DAVID walks to an upper level)

AUTHOR
A few had gotten there early, eager to make the grade. They thought they were alone when...

(DAVID begins to hum. The students look around)

STUDENT 1
Oh Jesus...you scared us, sir.

(DAVID just waves. STUDENT 1 walks to the platform. They talk in relative silence)

AUTHOR
While David and the student chatted, more of the scene crew arrived, eager to get started. They knew this show was going to be a beast, and they had no idea where to begin. Before long...

(STUDENT 1 returns)

STUDENT 1
Okay, I just talked with Mr. Payne. He told me where the scene plans are, what he needs each of you to...

STUDENT 2
Wait, you did what?

STUDENT 1
Mr. Payne told me to tell you...

(STUDENT 1 sees how they're looking at her)

STUDENT 1
What?

STUDENT 2
That's not funny.

STUDENT 1
It...wasn't supposed to be funny.

STUDENT 2
Mr. Payne's dead.

(Beat. STUDENT 1 laughs)

STUDENT 1
Oh. Of course he is.

STUDENT 2
I'm serious.

STUDENT 1
Yeah? Then who was I...?

STUDENT 2
He was hit by a car over break. Died instantly.

STUDENT 1
What?

(They look to where DAVID was standing. Nothing there)

AUTHOR
Within a few hours of accepting submissions for this project, I got my first one, from a young woman who had her own ghostly encounters at Elmhurst. I of course had to research the institution, the haunting, all of it. Imagine my surprise to discover that Mr. Payne graduated from Eastern Michigan University, where I now teach. And he was born and raised in Ypsilanti, where I...

(Beat. The other actors can tell the AUTHOR doesn't want to go on. THREE addresses the audience)

THREE

I was a senior at Elmhurst, playing Desdemona in "Othello" at the Mill Theatre. It's got an amazing history and is well-reputed for being EXTREMELY haunted. I'd had a few ghostly experiences prior to this—hearing someone walking around when I was the only one in the building; things being rearranged when I was out of a room; a piece of pipe falling onto the stage for no apparent reason—but this series of events was directed right at me.

(Lights/projections change to the small dressing room. THREE becomes DES, TWO becomes EM. They are walking in from rehearsal, reciting lines. A sheet is hung in such a way that a person can walk behind it, OR this can be a projection)

EM
How goes it now? He looks gentler than he did.

DES
He says he will return incontinent,
And hath demanded me to...

EM
Commanded.

DES
...go to...wait, what?

EM
Commanded. Not demanded.

(DES stares at her, uncertain)

EM
You've been saying it wrong for, like, a week.

(EM hands DES the script. DES finds the line)

DES
Oh son of a bitch.

EM
Told you.

DES
And he hath COMMANDED me to go to bed
And bid me to dismiss you.

EM
Dismiss me?

DES
It was his bidding. Therefore, good Emilia,
Give me my nightly wearing, and...

(Beat. DES is staring at her dressing room table)

EM
...and adieu.
We must not now displease him.

DES
No, I...I know the line. Just...

(She sits in a chair, suddenly exhausted)

EM
You ok?

DES
Yeah. Yeah, just...I don't know. I feel weird.

EM
You should sit down.

(Beat)

EM
Or, like, keep sitting down.

DES
Are you cold?

EM
This place is always cold. You'll get used to it.

DES
Not generally cold. Cold, here and now, just this second.

(Beat. EM rubs her hands)

EM
Maybe a little.

DES
I don't remember it being this cold in here before.

EM
It's an old building. And by "building," I mean "run down piece of crap."

(The heat pipes make a strange sound, almost like screaming. DES jumps)

EM
Exactly.

DES
Jesus! Is that what heat pipes are supposed to sound like?!

EM
Maybe I pissed it off. Sorry, Mill Theatre. You're not a piece of crap. You're very smart and pretty and you have a great personality.

(DES stands, begins to pack up her stuff)

EM
I thought we were gonna run lines.

DES
Let's go to my place.

EM
What will people say?

DES
I just...let's not do it here, ok?

EM
Yeah, sure. No problem.

(They put up costume pieces. A quiet humming is heard. The tune is decidedly odd)

EM
What's that?

DES
What's what?

EM
That thing you're humming. It's familiar...

DES
I...what?

(EM stares at her)

DES
I wasn't humming anything.

(As DES talks, the humming grows louder)

EM
Oh son of a...Caleb? Is that you!

DES
Sounds like a...

EM
He's totally screwing with us...

(She picks up a backstage headset)

EM
Here we go.

(She puts it on, talks into it)

EM
Hey, Caleb!

DES
Where the hell is it coming from?

EM
Reeeeeeeeeeeeeeeal funny, dude! Get off the headset
and go home, you dillweed.

(She detaches the cord from the headset)

EM
There. So endeth Caleb. Let's go.

*(The humming returns, louder. They both stare at the
headset. Without noticing it, the shape of a man appears
in silhouette, either on the screen or as a projection)*

DES
This is the soundboard ops, right? They're messing with us.

EM
Maybe?

DES
Caleb! Steve! This is immature even for you!

EM
I swear I saw them leave already.

DES
They live in the booth. They're laughing their asses off
right now.

EM
How...how about we just go, ok?

(EM grabs DES and starts to go. When they turn, they see the silhouette. They both scream and run out. When they leave, the ghost fades. THREE returns)

THREE
Yes, obviously I heard the theatre was haunted. Know what else is haunted? Every freaking theatre in America, if you listened to anyone who's worked in one. New theatres, theatres that have never had anyone die there... they'd have you believe it was two Poltergeists with a side of Ghostbusters. So yeah...it's cute to believe in those things, to keep the myth going, but "myth" was all I ever thought it was. I wish I could say that was the only weird thing that happened during that production. I wish I could. One night, during an actual performance...

(Othello begins)

DES
He says he will return incontinent—

(The audience laughs. EM rolls her eyes)

DES
He hath commanded me to go to bed,
And bade me to dismiss you.

EM
Dismiss me!

DES
It was his bidding. therefore, good Emilia,
Give me my nightly wearing, and adieu.
We must not now displease him.

(The humming begins again. Both can clearly hear it. Perhaps the silhouette returns. They are nervous but continue)

EM
I would you had never seen him!

DES
So would not I my love doth so approve him,
That even his stubbornness, his cheques, his frowns —
Prithee, unpin me, — have grace and favour in them.

EM
I have laid those sheets you bade me on the bed.

EM
Come, come you talk...

(A loud crash. Both freeze. THREE addresses the audience)

THREE
But I couldn't talk! A damn stage light had come crashing down from above! For what seemed like a hundred years, I just stood there, mouth open like a carp. The audience was holding their breath, no idea what to do. I finally snapped out of it and...so there's a ritual. A little thing we do at the Mill, and I'd never tried it, but...

EM
Ask him to stop.

THREE
He grew up in a different time...a time when manners were still a thing. And the actors, the professors...they all said that if you asked him to stop, he would.

EM
Come on...

DES
Mr. Payne...please just stop.

(Beat)

THREE
And the show went on without any more...distractions.
Our Emilia got the stage light off somehow and we just
went boldly forward. That night, the director smudged
the stage and we didn't have any problems again the rest
of the run.

*(ONE returns as AUTHOR, holding a smoldering smudge
stick. THREE breathes in deeply)*

THREE
I love that smell.

AUTHOR
Right?

THREE
White sage and...?

AUTHOR
Red cedar.

THREE
Nice.

AUTHOR
Smudging...a Native American tradition believed to be
cleansing, purifying. Emotions, psychic energy, spiritual
phenomenon.

(AUTHOR walks about the space, smudging the walls)

AUTHOR
You burn the herbs and rub the ash on the walls. Does
it work? Hell if I know. I will say this...when I was

twenty-five, my roommate and I moved into an apartment in Ypsilanti, Michigan. The first thing he did was
smudge all the walls in the house. After what happened
later...either he burned the wrong stuff, or smudging
doesn't work.

(A silhouette appears. A child, around ten years old)

AUTHOR
Later. It has to be later.

TWO
Now.

AUTHOR
No.

THREE
You have to tell it eventually.

AUTHOR
I'm building up to it, ok?

FOUR
You're scared.

AUTHOR
I'm not scared.

FOUR
You are.

AUTHOR
Shut up.

THREE
Maybe if you tell it, you'll stop being scared.

AUTHOR
Come on. You can't think it's that easy.

TWO
Maybe it is.

FOUR
Maybe it's time to…

AUTHOR
Please!

(They are silent)

AUTHOR
I said before that the Upper Peninsula seems to be, like, thirty-five percent ghosts. Anyone who's ever visited can sense it. A year before I began this project, I found an article about the "Ghost Towns of the Upper Peninsula." It focused on a series of towns that had all but disappeared due to the financial downturns in copper country. Or at least, that's what the article indicated. I decided I had to see it for myself. So in the summer of 2016, I drove to the northwestern UP and began my carefully planned tour. Here's what I learned: Don't trust advertising. Turns out the article wasn't written by a Michigander. I stayed in the first town on the list…Laurium. Was it a ghost town? No, it sure wasn't. It was a poor town, that's all. But still inhabited…hell, they even had a brand new hospital! Sure, most of the blocks were just empty storefronts, but…So I began my journey over the course of four days. Most of the towns were just like Laurium. They weren't the abandoned shells I was hoping to see, remnants of a time long past, now run down and full of…possibilities. But the towns weren't like that at all. Hell, two of them had gazebos! On beaches! With vacationers and…yeah, not ghost towns. At all. And then I found Mandan.

(Projection: The small road sign reading MANDAN)

AUTHOR
Saturday afternoon, I tracked down the third city on
my list...Mandan, Michigan. And by "track it down,"
I mean, "drove by it twice before I saw it." My GPS
was trying hard to tell me where to go, but even it was
confused. Finally, after circling a few times, I found that.

(AUTHOR points to the sign)

AUTHOR
Honest to god, THAT was the only sign, and if you blink
you miss it. And it's not on a road exactly, more like this
nearly-invisible path barely wide enough for a single
car. I'm a completist by nature. I had to check off every
city on my list, so into Mandan I went.

(Projection: Heavily forested path, a run-down building)

AUTHOR
THIS was a ghost town. No one lives in Mandan now. I
drove the narrow paths for thirty minutes, nearly blow-
ing my car's suspension while I did. These were not
maintained roads; these were just places where the grass
didn't grow. I found a grandtotal of two buildings in the
ruins, old houses that were most definitely not inhabited. Well, not in the conventional sense, anyway. I only
got out of my car once, to check out one of the buildings. I...didn't stay there long.

(Beat)

AUTHOR
Look, I don't really buy into ESP or whatnot. I mean,
maybe it's there, but I'm not the one who will convince
you of it. But when I was in Mandan, I...felt something.
I felt it the second I turned down that road, and when
I got out of the car...

(Beat)

AUTHOR
It wasn't a ghost. Not exactly. It was the town itself. That's what it felt like. Like…somehow, the ground and the buildings and the trees…like it was all part of something, a single consciousness. And it was angry. It did NOT want me there. There was something in the air itself…hostility. Offense. Me being there, me poking around, had pissed Mandan off. And I decided I had to turn around. As my old vehicle lurched up and down, that sense of anger grew worse and worse. I didn't even want to think what would happen if I got out of the car again. Finally, I found the main road again and put Mandan behind me. And believe me when I say I was NOT driving the speed limit.

(MANDAN fades away. The AUTHOR shakes away the feeling)

AUTHOR
The next story happened in the UP, in 1995. Foster City, Breen Township. A little unincorporated community on the east branch of the Sturgeon River. Used to be a big lumber town, but…well, sometimes as time marches on, it leaves some things behind.

(FOUR becomes COL)

FOUR
I live in Marquette, which my mom calls the L.A. of the UP. Which…fine. It's a nice town. The biggest town north of the Bridge. But like every town here, you don't have to go far to find wilderness.

(FOUR looks to AUTHOR)

FOUR
I need a car.

AUTHOR
What?

FOUR
I need a car. For the scene.

AUTHOR
What kind of budget do you think we have? Use those.

(AUTHOR points to onstage blocks or chairs)

FOUR
No steering wheel?

(AUTHOR glares at FOUR. FOUR sits, with THREE becoming CAROL)

COL
That's my mom's friend Carol. Carol was born and bred in Illinois. Now the Land of Lincoln can seem a lot like most Midwest states, but none of them are anything like the UP.

CAROL
Wisconsin is. It's connected to the Peninsula too.

(Beat)

COL
So when Carol decided to visit, I knew we had to give her the grand tour.

CAROL
How long could it take?

COL
It isn't Rhode Island, Carol. You can't just walk across it.

CAROL
With enough provisions, you can walk across anything.

COL
I...fine.

(The projection shows a variety of locales in the UP)

COL
I took her to the Adventure Mines. Guided tours through this huge old copper mine.

CAROL
Fun fact: That's literally the name the mine had back in the day. It wasn't to sell it to tourists or anything. The company that owned it was literally the Adventure Mining Company. Literally.

COL
Literally?

CAROL
Literally.

COL
We took a shipwreck tour.

CAROL
Oh my god. Like, shipwrecks...you think pirate ships in the Caribbean. But we're on this glass-bottomed boat and...oh my god. The Kiowa. The Manhattan. The Smith Moore.

COL
It's pretty cool.

CAROL
SO COOL.

COL
And of course, I had to buy her a pastie.

CAROL
Dear god. Twelve hundred calories in a pastry shell.

COL
It's a tradition.

CAROL
(*Whispering to the audience*) I didn't poop for a week.

COL
Then near the end of her trip, Carol said to me...

CAROL
I want to see the houses! Let's go find some cool houses!

COL
The architecture of the UP is something to behold, even the rundown stuff. There's a lot of Victorian style places. You see, these mining magnates and the lumber barons would build these huge, gorgeous mansions for their families. Some of them...my god...it's like they flew over from Europe and just dropped down here. And of course the foremen would build their own places nearby, and the next thing you know, you had a city.

CAROL
Of course, that's while the mines were booming.

COL
They...didn't boom forever.

CAROL
No they did not. The Empire Mine, Cliff Mine, Central Mine, Quincy Mine...

COL
More mines than you could believe.

CAROL
I kind of picture the UP as entirely hollowed out under the surface.

COL
The mines close, but the houses remain. And Carol wanted to see them. So we drove. Houghton…

CAROL
You wouldn't believe it. It was like all these little mansions in a row, old as hell but people still living in them.

COL
Laurium.

CAROL
I saw a house there that was basically the Addams Family house. Swear to god. I was waiting for Lurch to pop up.

COL
We drove around for hours…until we ended up in Foster City.

(Projection of Foster City)

COL
A small town that's now home to two churches, a Christmas tree farm, and the Post Office, but it was once the largest town in the Upper Peninsula.

CAROL
The logging industry, ya know?

COL
In 1995, Foster was so remote that no TV station could even reach there; same with cable. You had a VCR or nothing.

CAROL
Colleen took us to this cute little restaurant the...shit, what was it...

COL
The Milltown Inn.

CAROL
Yes! Right! And we got ourselves some Swedish pancakes and just started talking to folks, getting the history, you know?

COL
Well, turns out Foster City was basically built by the Lord of Lumber himself, Swan Peterson.

CAROL
He owned the mill at first, and in 1925 he literally bought the whole town.

COL
He outlawed alcohol in Foster City...and it's STILL outlawed!

CAROL
It's true! There's a couple little bars just over the city limits, but that's it.

COL
It's almost like he didn't want huge, flannel-clad dudes swinging axes while plastered.

CAROL
Well, it turned out that back in the day, he had this gorgeous old house.

COL
The guy owned the town. You better believe he had the best place around.

CAROL
And sure enough, the folks at the Milltown told us right
how to get there.

COL
So...off we went.

(Projection of an old manor house)

COL
It...took some doing to find the place.

CAROL
It was hidden in the woods.

COL
Again, not an unusual thing in the UP. But...when we
were driving through the woods, I felt something.

CAROL
I didn't.

COL
I know you didn't, but I did.

CAROL
Okay.

COL
Just...there are places in the world that don't feel like
the present ever reached them. Like it hit this specific
point in the past and just...stopped.

CAROL
I didn't feel that.

COL
Carol, you're killing me.

*(CAROL is silent. Old music, as though from an old
music box plays)*

COL
Finally, we found this paved driveway. Out there, in all those trees, pavement wasn't what I was expecting. But there it was. We followed it for quite a way, until we saw…it.

CAROL
It was beautiful.

COL
It really was. Like a huge white flower growing up among the trees.

CAROL
A true, old Victorian. And no modernizations.

COL
No TV antennas or new garages or porch lights or anything like that. It was from a different time.

CAROL
I wanted to stop.

COL
You wanted to go inside.

CAROL
I did. I did want to go inside.

COL
The folks at the Milltown told us no one lived there anymore.

CAROL
So what's the harm?

COL
The harm is walking into an old house and falling through rotten floorboards. Or getting tetanus. Or finding a bear.

CAROL
There aren't bears up here.

COL
There are absolutely bears up here.

(Beat. CAROL stares at her)

CAROL
Really?

COL
One hundred percent.

CAROL
I still really wanted to look inside.

COL
We argued about this as we drove around the house. Just as we were finishing our circle...I saw her.

(Projection: A window on the house. Slowly, the image of an old woman appears in it. It is hard to see her face as her hair is in front of it)

COL
Oh hell!

CAROL
What?! What is it!?

COL
Look!

(COL points)

CAROL
Is that...?

COL
Somebody freaking lives here!

CAROL
I thought they said...

COL
They were screwing with us! We've been out here like a couple of creepers and...

CAROL
She's got to be ninety years old!

COL
Still want to go inside?

CAROL
No, I do not.

(CAROL waves at the woman, speaks as though she can be heard)

CAROL
Sorry, ma'am! Sorry! We didn't know!

COL
God, she's looking right at us.

(Projection: The woman fades)

COL
Ok, time to go.

CAROL
What if we asked her if we could look around?

COL
Nope.

CAROL
I mean, we're already here.

COL
(To audience) But I couldn't hear Carol anymore. We

were just coming around the side of the house, back to the long driveway, and....

(Projection: The woman is now in front of the house, staring at them)

CAROL
OH MY GOD!

COL
(To audience) She had been on the third floor, ok. The third floor of this freaking massive mansion. And then three seconds later...there. Ground floor, on the porch, just...staring at us.

CAROL
What the hell!?

COL
An Olympic sprinter couldn't have made that run. How the hell did this old lady do it?

CAROL
Go! GO GO GO!

COL
But I froze. I admit it. She was staring at us...and I was staring at her. I couldn't understand what I was seeing.

(CAROL shakes COL)

CAROL
Colleen! We have to go!

COL
I came to. I didn't get any of this, but I suddenly knew I didn't want to be here anymore. I turned around, ready to head to the driveway and...

(TWO appears, dressed as the old woman. She is in front

of the car, several feet away, staring at them. She fades from the projection)

CAROL
Colleen...

COL
There. Right in front of us.

CAROL
Colleen!

COL
It was impossible. I knew it was impossible. But the old woman was IN the driveway, looking right at us!

CAROL
GO!

(They drive, jerking the wheel. TWO exits quickly)

COL
I floored it, swerving out of her way. That instinct just kicked in...get around this woman and get the hell out. I turned around to make sure I hadn't hit her and...gone. She was just gone.

CAROL
Oh my god.

COL
I thought Carol was looking at the same place, the now empty spot on the driveway. She wasn't.

CAROL
Colleen...look...

(CAROL points behind them. Projection of the window. The old woman is back in the window. She slowly raises her hand as if saying goodbye, then pulls the curtain closed)

COL
I drove us straight home...going about ninety the whole way.

CAROL
I never found out who that old woman was.

COL
I never wanted to know. But I'll tell you this for free... we never went back.

(AUTHOR returns as they reset the stage. Projection of a Michigan autumn. He's perhaps wearing a Halloween mask)

AUTHOR
Halloween in the Midwest...it's different here than it is in other places. I think part of it is we live in a part of the country that has a real autumn. Seriously...Georgia, California, Florida...try trick-or-treating when it's eighty-five degrees at night, under palm trees. It's NOT the same. But here...oh yeah. You know what I'm talking about. You've all experienced it. The chilly air, the sound of the wind through the corn stalks...

(The sound of wind through corn stalks)

AUTHOR
...And everything smelling like apples and wood smoke. You know it and you love it. Wisconsin, Michigan, Ohio, Illinois...they're farming states, and Halloween is a harvest holiday. There are rituals, some across the board, some unique to the individual.

THREE
Hayrides. Haunted hayrides.

TWO
And corn mazes.

THREE
Yes. Absolutely.

FOUR
It isn't October until I've had my apple cider donut.

TWO
Oh god, the cider.

THREE
Gallons of it.

FOUR
Lakes of it.

TWO
We're the Great Lakes state, right? Gimme a lake of cider!

AUTHOR
And horror movies.

FOUR
Obviously horror movies.

AUTHOR
I love screamers. If you become a die-hard horror fan, the downside is you just don't scare all that easily. You get...not desensitized but familiar with it. And sadly, the familiar just isn't all that scary. That's where having a screamer is vital.

(The chairs are set up as movie theatre seats. "Night of the Living Dead" is projected. THREE & FOUR sit, watching it. THREE is clearly not scared, but FOUR is petrified)

AUTHOR
There are movies you've watched a hundred times, that you can quote every single line from, and you still don't

get sick of it. The problem with horror movies is that even though you love it, the scare will never quite be the same as the first time. The solution? Experience the scare all over again through a screamer.

(FOUR curls into themselves)

AUTHOR
A screamer is a very specific type of person. They like horror...hell, some of them even love horror...but they never lose their fear response. They jump, they run... they scream. Step one: Introduce them to a film they haven't seen yet.

THREE
This actually ran during Saturday afternoons, see, because in 1968...

FOUR
Shhh.

THREE
...horror movies were geared towards teenagers. But there wasn't a rating system really at the time so...

FOUR
Shhh!

THREE
...these kids had no idea they'd be seeing zombies tearing people apart and eating them!

FOUR
SHHH!

THREE
Sorry, sorry.

AUTHOR
Step two: Watch them, watch their reactions. Remember:

You know this film, and they do not. You know when the scares are coming. They do not. Observe. Study. Prepare.

(Projection: The "They're coming to get you, Barbara" scene)

FOUR
Oh god...it's right there! Why aren't they running!?

THREE
They don't know it's a zombie.

FOUR
Look at it! Just look!

THREE
They can't hear you, honey.

FOUR
Oh god oh god oh god...

AUTHOR
Step three: The pounce. The pounce depends entirely on your sense of timing. Too soon, and they'll jump but they'll miss the actual moment in the film. Too late, and the scare has already floated away. But if you time it juuust right...

(The moment when the zombie attacks Johnny. THREE grabs FOUR by the shoulders. FOUR shrieks)

AUTHOR
Oh yeah. That's the stuff.

(FOUR hits THREE while THREE laughs)

FOUR
You suck!

THREE
So good! SO GOOD!

FOUR
YOU FREAKING SUCK!

(They begin to set up the next scene)

AUTHOR
You see, with a screamer beside you, you can re-experience the moments that would otherwise be lost to you. That's why they're so damn important. A good screamer is worth their weight in gold.

FOUR
I will murder you.

THREE
Promises, promises.

AUTHOR
I think at the end of the day, fear wants to be a shared experience. Not only because there's safety in numbers, but...solitude creates doubt. You become unsure of what you've seen, if you've even seen anything at all. And all of a sudden, you dismiss the experience that left you completely terrified as "just your imagination."

(The window from earlier is projected. Moonlight pours through it)

AUTHOR
The thing I saw...the THINGS I've seen...I was alone. And to this day, I still don't know. I would've given anything to have someone there, someone I could grab and say...

(AUTHOR grabs TWO)

AUTHOR
This thing I'm seeing, are you seeing it too!?

(TWO stares at AUTHOR, then moves along)

AUTHOR
See? Safety in numbers.

(TWO becomes ROOMMATE)

TWO
Hey, check this out!

(Projection: An apartment in a reconfigured house)

AUTHOR
In 2002, my roommate and I moved to Ypsilanti. We were renting the upstairs of a home that had been broken up into smaller apartments. You know the kind. We were thrilled, loved the house. A couple of young punks ready for anything. It was the middle of the summer when we moved in. I'd drawn the short straw and got the smaller of the two bedrooms. So while I was setting my stuff up, I heard...

ROOMMATE
Dude, seriously! Look at this!

AUTHOR
I assumed it was gonna be another round of "Look at my huuuuge room." But when I got there...

TWO
Weird, right?

(TWO rolls on a free standing door, perhaps four feet high)

AUTHOR
What is that?

ROOMMATE
It's like a little closet, I think. There's a small room back there.

AUTHOR
Huh.

ROOMMATE
Wanna see the freaky part?

AUTHOR
...do I?

(TWO opens the door. A small bolt lock can be seen on the inside)

AUTHOR
Is that...it looks like a deadbolt.

ROOMMATE
Yeah. On the inside of the door.

(Beat)

ROOMMATE
So...why the hell would someone need to lock themselves inside a closet?

(Beat)

AUTHOR
All of a sudden, I was totally fine with having the small room.

(TWO messes with the deadbolt)

ROOMMATE
...not like an adult could even get in there. Really just kid-sized...

AUTHOR
On our first day in that house, we found something... unsettling. I wish that was where it had ended.

(Beat)

AUTHOR
We found what we found by accident. But there are those who do this for a living. Well, "living" might be a stretch but...ghost hunters. Paranormal investigators. Psychic detectives. These are the brave folks who take their love of all things spectral one step further. Or maybe many steps. Some operate individually, others form organizations. The Midwest Ghost Society. Spirit World Paranormal Investigators. Psychics Unite. Every state in the Great Lakes area has no fewer than a dozen such organizations. Now before you buy a jumpsuit and a proton pack, please know...this is what is called pseudoscience. Seriously. In 2002, the National Science Foundation identified ghost hunting practices "among pseudoscientific beliefs." So when I got a submission from one such paranormal investigator...obviously I had to put it in the play.

(Projection. A ghost hunting team)

AUTHOR
This submission came in late, but it was too good to pass up. The submitter asked for total anonymity, so I'm going to call her, if it really was a her...Sue. Let's call her organization the...Strange Happenings Investigative Team. I cannot emphasize enough how much no group of that name exists. Skeptical as I am, this story just leapt out at me. I'll let Sue explain...

(FOUR becomes SUE)

SUE
Sue? Really?

AUTHOR
For pseudonym.

(Beat. FOUR just stares at him)

AUTHOR
Come on. That's hilarious.

SUE
You're the worst.

(SUE addresses the audience)

SUE
So here's the thing...we're not weirdos. WE'RE NOT. People hear "paranormal investigator" and they immediately think we go into trances and worship crystals and live in our parents' basements. That's not us. Not...most of us. We're normal people you see in the supermarket. We have regular jobs. I actually work at a bookstore in Green Bay. What we are are people who are curious about what comes after. We believe something does. It may not be quantifiable YET, but neither was Radium until 1898.

AUTHOR
Poor Marie Curie.

SUE
I knoooow. So sad. Anyway, it's important to understand that we're not fruitcakes. We take this very seriously because we truly do hope that one day, science will know what to make of this.

(THREE becomes MEG)

MEG
One common misconception is that we get called in on a lot of cases.

SUE
This is Meg. We're partners with...

(She doesn't want to say it. AUTHOR urges her on)

SUE
...Strange Happenings Investigative Team.

MEG
We do get them on occasion, but they're usually nothing.

SUE
Faulty wiring.

MEG
Something in the HVAC unit.

SUE
But people watch these terrible TV shows now. Ghost Hunters, Ghost Adventures...a bunch of bros totally stoked on how awesome they are. They find ghosts everywhere...because they have to. Because it's TV.

MEG
What we usually do is seek out sightings ourselves. Most towns have their popular haunted building. Old hotel.

SUE
Train stations.

MEG
Abandoned mental hospital.

SUE
Oh those are the best!

MEG
Right? Like, remember that one in Clark County?

SUE
Um, yes. It was incredible.

MEG
So incredible.

SUE
So we do our research. Local folklore is a good start. Some web searching. And if we find a site or a legend that seems really interesting, we bring it to the team.

MEG
If we agree it's worth checking out, we follow proper procedure.

SUE
We're not barbarians.

MEG
We reach out to the owners of the site, if there are any, to get permission. If we need to coordinate with local authorities, we do that too.

SUE
Visitation permits, liability waivers...it's a lot of paper-work.

MEG
But sometimes, it's as simple as getting permission to stay past closing. That's what it was like at Riverside Cemetery in Appleton, Wisconsin.

AUTHOR
It happened in a cemetery! A cemetery! It was like I struck gold!

(Beat)

AUTHOR
Please continue.

(Projection: The Riverside Cemetery)

SUE
Meg and I were assigned to investigate this one. It was our find, after all. I've been to Appleton plenty of times,

and it didn't take long to hear the story of Kate Blood.

AUTHOR
Hand to god, that was her real name. Kate. BLOOD.
COME ON!

MEG
Sir. Are we going to have to ask you to leave?

(Beat)

AUTHOR
I'll be good.

SUE
There have been many, many stories about Kate Blood,
the ghost who haunts Riverside Cemetery. The common
story is that she murdered her husband and children
with an axe before committing suicide.

(Projection: Kate's tombstone)

MEG
That one's easy to dismiss, as the tombstone indicates he
survived her by forty-two years.

SUE
She's been everything from a witch to an axe murderer
to a ghost, so we decided to investigate ourselves. With
permission from the groundskeeper.

MEG
Our research indicated she was in fact much loved in
her community.

SUE
This would've been late 1800s.

MEG
She was a religious volunteer, and her husband was one

of the town founders. But...she was only twenty-three when she contracted tuberculosis.

SUE
She even moved to Kansas, in hope that the dry air would slow its progress. It didn't.

MEG
When she died, her body was shipped back to Appleton, where she was interred. Her obituary read...

(AUTHOR takes a paper from his desk and reads)

AUTHOR
"She lived for others, and for those she loved, no sacrifice was too great which involved their happiness."

SUE
When we got there, the caretaker walked us through...

(TWO becomes the CARETAKER. They are now in the scene. A gravestone appears)

CARETAKER
See, it's tricky because her grave is quite a bit away from the rest of the cemetery. Hell if I know why.

MEG
Like their own private plot.

SUE
What were those things in the woods? Those stone things.

CARETAKER
The stone grottos? That's what I call 'em. Folks say they used to be for satanic worship or something. But I'm pretty sure they used to have little statues of saints in 'em.

SUE
But you don't know for sure?

CARETAKER
Nope. Now you're not gonna mess with this or anything, right?

SUE
Absolutely not.

CARETAKER
'Cause this grave gets a lot of visitors. Most are nice enough, put a flower on it and all, but some mess with the stone. Disrespectful, and I'm the one who has to clean it up.

MEG
We're just gonna take a couple readings with our equipment, and stick around for a while.

SUE
See if we see anything.

CARETAKER
Well, you picked a good night for it. Full moon's comin' up. That's when they say things get...weird.

MEG
That's what we're hoping.

CARETAKER
Well, you two have fun, I guess.

(CARETAKER walks off, muttering to herself)

CARETAKER
...buncha weirdos...

MEG
Ready?

SUE
Let's do this.

(SUE addresses the audience while MEG sets up small bits of equipment)

SUE
So there are a few things we usually encounter in a real haunting. Cold spots, when an area gets much colder than everywhere around it.

MEG
Orbs, which are small balls of light usually only seen through photo images.

(MEG checks her camera)

SUE
Electronic Voice Phenomena, which allows us to pick up trace voices of the spirits.

AUTHOR
More on that later.

SUE
But the beauty of a haunting is...there's always something that makes it unique. Moving shadows, floating objects...

MEG
I've actually seen a medium channel a spirit and communicate with automatic writing. It blew my mind!

SUE
The point is, whatever preparation we make, we always have to stay on our feet.

MEG
Hence, lots and lots of coffee.

(MEG hands SUE a thermos of coffee)

SUE
Yes, we went on the night of the full moon. Multiple stories indicate that Kate becomes most active under the full moon.

MEG
We always ALWAYS take folk legends with a grain of salt. But what the hell, ya know?

SUE
So we waited and we waited. And drank a LOT of coffee.

(SUE puts some printouts in front of them. They discuss as they wait. PROJECTION: a full moon)

MEG
So I think we can safely rule out axe-murderer, yeah?

SUE
One hundred percent.

MEG
Death by consumption. That's the thing where you cough yourself bloody, right?

SUE
Yeah. Basically turns your lungs into soup.

MEG
Ugh. Gross. EMF detecting anything?

(SUE checks a small device)

SUE
Nope.

MEG
Dammit, it's past midnight.

SUE
Almost like ghosts don't have a sense of the dramatic.

MEG
Wanna call it a night?

SUE
Sure. I think I saw a Denny's when we drove in.

MEG
Yes. I need pancakes.

(As SUE rises, she puts her hand on the tombstone to steady herself. She yelps and immediately pulls back)

SUE
AH! DAMMIT!

MEG
You ok?

SUE
I think I burned my hand!

MEG
What?

SUE
Hand! Burned!

MEG
On what?

(They stare at the tombstone)

MEG
No way.

SUE
Touch it.

MEG
Absolutely not.

SUE
We need to know if it's just me or...

(Beat)

SUE
You know you want to.

(MEG hesitantly touches the stone, then immediately pulls her hand back)

MEG
Holy crap!

SUE
Yeah?

MEG
It's hot! Like left-the-stove-on-too-long hot!

SUE
Ok, that...get the camera!

MEG
What?

SUE
I wanna see if we get any orbs! Take some pictures! Now!

MEG
Right right right.

(MEG grabs a camera and takes quick photos. SUE does the same with her cellphone. After a bit—)

SUE
Ok. That...that was awesome.

MEG
I bet we got something. I bet we did!

(SUE checks her phone pics)

SUE
Nothing here, but I bet you got something.

MEG
They are not gonna believe us when we tell them.

SUE
Oh, they'll believe. Especially if some orbs show up...

MEG
You wanna stick around for a bit more, see if anything happens?

SUE
I absolutely do.

(MEG picks up her coffee, stares at the tombstone)

SUE
What?

MEG
Just...kinda wondering.

SUE
If the tombstone will warm up your coffee?

MEG
No.

(Beat)

MEG
Yes.

SUE
Just...is that disrespectful?

MEG
For science!

(MEG puts the thermos on the stone. Waits)

SUE
I don't know about this.

MEG
Future generations will thank us.

(She takes the thermos)

MEG
Moment of truth.

(She drinks)

SUE
Well?

MEG
Still normal temperature.

(SUE stops, stares at MEG. Her teeth are red)

MEG
What?

SUE
Holy shit...Meg...

MEG
What?!

(SUE holds her phone camera up to MEG)

MEG
I...oh my god, is that blood?

(SUE grabs the thermos and looks in, then immediately shuts it. She looks ill)

MEG
What the hell is going on!?

SUE
We should go.

MEG
Is there like an emergency room nearby or…

SUE
We'll find one! Let's go!

(As they grab their items, blood starts to trickle out of the tombstone)

MEG
Go! Now!

SUE
Wait, let me just…

(SUE tries to take pics of the tombstone, but MEG is pulling her away)

MEG
NOW!

(They exit. AUTHOR enters, reading the end of the submission)

AUTHOR
"By the time we got to the emergency room, the blood… or whatever it was…was gone. The coffee was just coffee again. They looked at us like we were nuts, but we saw what we saw. Unfortunately, the photos were not helpful."

(Projection: Badly blurred photos)

AUTHOR
"I wish we'd gotten something more tangible but that's how it sometimes goes with these investigations."

(AUTHOR folds up the paper)

AUTHOR
Safety in numbers doesn't necessarily mean sanity in numbers.

(Projection: An 1800s séance)

AUTHOR
In the late 1800s, the European craze over spiritual-ism had made its way to America. Séances, clairvoy-ance, psychic phenomena…if it involved communing with the dead, Americans wanted in. The wealthy hired mediums to contact departed loved ones. A bizarre trend called "table-turning parties" took place, in which a seer would be invited to a home and…well, here.

(AUTHOR sets up a small table. The others join him)

THREE
What do we do?
AUTHOR
Just put your fingertips on the table.

(They do so. Beat)

FOUR
This is thrilling.

AUTHOR
Obviously there's more to it than that.

TWO
There'd have to be.

AUTHOR
What you'd do is…the medium would read the alphabet. A, B, C, D…

(On D, the table tilts)

AUTHOR
There! See how the table tilted? They believed that spirits could spell out words, even full sentences this way,
by tipping the table when they got to the right letters.
You see...

THREE
It's a Ouija board.

AUTHOR
Not exactly.

THREE
It's basically a Ouija board.

AUTHOR
It's...let's call it a predecessor to the Ouija board.

TWO
People had parties for this?

AUTHOR
It was spiritualism! This was just the main event! There
were hors d'oeuvres, and drinks, and...

FOUR
Yeah, there better be drinks.

AUTHOR
I'm just saying...things like this were happening all over
the country! Even...here!

(Projection: The old Morris Pratt Institute)

AUTHOR
Back in the day, it wasn't enough to just be a medium.
You wanted to be an accredited medium. And so the
Morris Pratt Institute was born.

(Projection: Morris Pratt)

AUTHOR
A devoted follower of the Spiritualism movement, old Morrie had made his fortune following a mystic's advice about where to set up a mine. Said site became the extremely lucrative Ashwood Mine of Ironwood, MI, and Mr. Pratt always said, "If I am made rich, I will give part of it to Spiritualism." Well, he was made very rich, so he bought up a grand building in his hometown of Whitewater, Wisconsin. He converted said building into a proper school and chapel, and brought in many renowned professors to train would-be table-tippers. Rules were established for proper spirit summoning. No actual degrees could be earned there, but the train-ing...They offered everything from gen-eds to Psychic Research and "The Bible as it Pertains to Spiritualism Beliefs." By 1917, the halls were overrun by a total of twenty-five students, predominantly from the Midwest. It should be noted that the serious paranormal classes were NOT open to the public. If you wanted to pull ectoplasm out of thin air, you had to be a full-timer. Now the town itself never really got onboard with this Institute of Ghostly Learning. As the years went on and Spiritualism went out of fashion, so too did Morris Pratt's dream. Enrollment died out, and the school was eventually shut down in 1946. But do you really think a Spiritualism school would really stay dead?

(Projection: The current Morris Pratt Institute)

AUTHOR
The Morris Pratt Institute was reborn in Milwaukee in the Sixties, as a member of the National Spiritualist Association of Churches. AND it remains active even today! Now a correspondence school, run by a board of trustees, you too can enroll and gain certification over thirty lessons, including Spiritualism as Science,

The Theory of Healing, and A Study of Phenomena. I'm not saying I sent off for their reading materials…but I'm not NOT saying it either.

(Projection fades)

AUTHOR
During my travels, I couldn't help but notice the Midwest's fascination with the eerie…I mean "weird stuff", not the lake. The Institute was just one instance. But if you just scratch the surface of this region, you'll find more than you bargained for. From the creepy catacombs underneath the City Market of Indianapolis…

(Projection of City Market Catacombs)

AUTHOR
…to Ohio's haunted battlefield Ft. Meigs…

(Projection of Ft. Meigs)

AUTHOR
The Midwest loves the weird, the bizarre, and the haunted, and they love it all the year 'round. Even if that fascination takes them straight to Hell.

(Projection: Hell, Michigan)

AUTHOR
See what I did there? Welcome to Hell…a cute little town about fifteen miles north of Ann Arbor. Now "cute" is in the eye of the beholder, but this beholder found it fascinating. What started out as a grist mill and general store on the banks of Hell Creek has become a full-blown tourist attraction.

(As the author describes places, the projections change to them)

AUTHOR
The Hellhole Diner, the Creamatory of Screams, Putt-Putt golf, kayaking down Hell Creek…even a wedding chapel! That's right, you can get legally married…in Hell! As they advertise, "a marriage that starts in Hell has no place to go but up!" And every year, they host the annual Hearsefest…an auto show all their own, featuring exactly what you think. Hearses of all makes and models show up while the participants cook up hotdogs and hamburgers on casket grills. Prizes are awarded for "Scariest Hearse," "Best Casket Cart," and the ever popular "How the Hell did it make it here?"

(A strange device on the desk begins to beep. AUTHOR picks it up)

AUTHOR
This fella here? This is an EMF detector. Stands for electromagnetic field. This gets explained in every ghost-based movie and tv show in a desperate attempt to show juuust how smart the writers really are. I hate that crap…stating common knowledge like you're in a special club passing off hidden secrets to the poor, ignorant masses. "Well, Halloween was in fact originally a pagan holiday called Samhain…" YES! WE KNOW! Everyone knows that! That isn't fancy information, you're just an elitist nerd who wants to feel important!

(Beat. The others stare at the AUTHOR. AUTHOR collects himself, holds out the device)

AUTHOR
So you see, ghosts are rumored to cause disruptions in the electromagnetic field, and a device like this can register those sudden changes. So yeah, it's a common tool used in ghost hunting. So is this…

(AUTHOR holds out a tape recorder)

AUTHOR
I know. You're all gasping in awe at this mighty tape recorder. But believe it or not, this is the basis of some much more sophisticated technology...technology which can be used to capture EVP. Ghost hunters do love their acronyms. EVP stands for electronic voice Phenomenon. Maybe you've heard of that too. What you do is set up in a room that's supposedly haunted, get all the equipment ready, then start asking questions. Lots of questions. Sometimes over and over. You record the entire conversation...because even if you don't hear any responses, it may in fact be a conversation. You then go back and start playing the tape...and listening. And if you're lucky, you may hear...

(A strange electronic sound that may be a voice)

AUTHOR
Hardly clear, right? It sometimes takes some scrubbing to make it all out, but that's what EVP sounds like. Sometimes a voice, sometimes...

(More EVP. This sounds like horrible screams)

AUTHOR
Yeah...it'll get under your skin.

(AUTHOR holds both items)

AUTHOR
EMF detector, tape recorder. Who needs proton packs when you have...?

(The EMF detector starts to make noise)

AUTHOR
...huh...

(AUTHOR hits the device. It stops)

AUTHOR
I'm…choosing to ignore that. So yes, when a group of folks decide to track down the paranorm…

(The EMF detector goes off again)

AUTHOR
…dammit…

(Projection: A moonlit bedroom. AUTHOR just stares at it)

AUTHOR
Fine.

(Beat)

AUTHOR
My roommate and I had been living in the house for maybe six months when the first…event happened. I feel like I have to say right off the bat…for a lot of my life, I had night terrors. They're these really intense nightmares in which your body becomes physically involved…you start to act out the nightmare. And when you wake up from it, the nightmare doesn't just stop. There's a few minutes where…your eyes are wide open, and you're seeing both reality AND the dream super-imposed over each other. It's unnerving to say the least.

(The EMF detector goes off again)

AUTHOR
OK, OK! Damn. So about six months in, what I saw…I was asleep. The bedroom window was at the foot of my bed, and it faced the moon, so I'd always get this pale light washing over me. Anyway, I was lying in bed, awake or asleep I don't even know, and I realized I couldn't

move. I guess it's called sleep paralysis, but all I knew was that my limbs were frozen solid. And I knew I wasn't alone. I knew it.

(The three actors enter in robes and hoods)

AUTHOR
They were wearing robes and hoods. They weren't moving, not at first. They were just standing around the bed, staring down at me. I couldn't see their faces. Then suddenly, one of them raised their arms...

(One of them raises their arms)

AUTHOR
...and in their hands, a snake.

(Projection: A writhing snake)

AUTHOR
I wanted to scream. I wanted to run out of the room and down the stairs and into the streets, but I was completely immobile. Then, the robed thing, the one holding the snake...

(It drops its hands. The snake disappears)

AUTHOR
It dropped the snake right onto me. And suddenly, just like that, I could move. I screamed at the top of my lungs and leapt out of the bed. I tore my blankets off, looking for the snake...I knew it was there...I knew it!

(The room lights up)

AUTHOR
Nothing. It was just my bedroom, totally normal, no hooded people, no snake, no nothing. But...it sounds dumb, but it felt like they were still there. It took me an hour to shake that feeling.

(AUTHOR puts down the items)

AUTHOR
I guess if I'd really shaken it, we wouldn't be here right now.

(Projection: a nice house)

AUTHOR
When I was accepting stories for this project, there were of course things I was hoping to find. I mean, I knew the chances of finding spontaneous combustion or bleeding walls were pretty slim, but I still held out hope for something really...eerie. The kind of thing that just chills you, that...it's that feeling when you absolutely know you should look away, and you absolutely can't.

(Beat)

AUTHOR
It was literally the last submission I got. From Toledo, Ohio...

(TWO becomes MELODY)

MELODY
Thing about living in a haunted house...well, a thing. There's definitely more than one thing...is that people are...reluctant to believe you. Human nature, right? That's why we had to have proof.

(MELODY takes the recorder)

MELODY
The things that happened in my house...it wasn't a one-time event. It got so bad, in fact, that...yeah, we actually brought in a priest to bless the house when I was little. It didn't help. It...did the opposite of helping. The spirits...

(Beat)

MELODY
That's right. Spirits, plural. There were two. A girl...

(FOUR becomes the FEMALE GHOST)

MELODY
... a teenage girl with long dark hair and a long white dress/nightgown. The other...the guy.

(Beat)

MELODY
Our contact with him was less. And I cannot express how glad I am for that. He wasn't hostile like you might think...no bleeding walls or breaking windows. But there was a sense of...menace to him. I think it was menace? I...

(The lights dim a good bit. FEMALE puts on glow in the dark gloves and mask. MELODY remains lit)

MELODY
The girl made the most appearances. She was...mischievous, curious...irritable. She picked on my brother more than the rest of us. Flicking his ear, throwing things at him when he was in the garage. He smoked out there.

(The sound of cans slamming against a wall)

MELODY
One time he opened the garage, and he just saw her hands and face coming right at him.

(FEMALE runs at the audience, only her face and hands glowing)

MELODY
But she wasn't always hostile. Sometimes she was just... sad.

(FEMALE sits on the chair, holding a flashlight)

MELODY
One day, he came into the garage and she was sitting in the car, in the driver's seat.

(FEMALE turns on the light, as if lit by the dashboard)

MELODY
She wasn't looking at him. She wasn't looking at anything. She was just staring out, like there was something she could see that we couldn't. My mom thinks she wanted to leave and was jealous that we could come and go in that car any time, and she was trapped there.

(FEMALE turns off her light and exits)

MELODY
The guy...or...we always thought it was a guy, but it never made itself that clear. None of us ever got a good look at him. I came the closest, and what I saw...

(Lights on a bed, or something that could be used as a bed. As MELODY speaks, she gets into the bed)

MELODY
I was eight years old, just a kid really. I'd only just started to understand that we weren't alone in the house. But when you're little like that, a ghost? That's not scary; that's awesome! I so badly wanted to meet the girl in the garage. Even now, I wonder if that...desire, whatever it was, is what drew him to me.

(The room goes dark, as if lit by a night-light)

MELODY
It was fall. I remember because school hadn't been going long. Oh, and the window was open. Even as a kid, I loved cold air when I slept. Which...maybe that's

why I didn't feel him come in. But he was there. And I knew beyond all doubt that this was NOT the thing my brother had seen.

(The sound of footsteps in the room)

MELODY
The steps were heavy, way too heavy to be my mom. And they were slow, deliberate.

(MELODY looks around. The steps stop. She lies back down. A few seconds later, they start back up)

MELODY
It was circling the room, whatever it was. I thought maybe it didn't know I was there, maybe it would just leave. It didn't.

(The sound of creaking bed springs)

MELODY
I felt the foot of my bed sink in, like someone was sitting on it. Someone big. I was...terrified is too small a word. Have you ever been so scared that you're just completely frozen, paralyzed? That's what it was. I couldn't see this thing, but it was there, lurking. I don't know what made me think of it but...I always slept with a night-light on, and I wondered...just because I couldn't see this thing didn't mean...

(Light is projected on the wall. We see the shadow of a large man. He turns and looks at MELODY, who jumps up and runs out of the scene)

MELODY
I slept in my mom's room that night. And for the next week. The next day, she called the priest from St. Pat's. He came in, said some things in Latin, splashed some holy water around, and left. But he was the only one

who left.

(The sound of doors slamming)

MELODY
The ghosts got agitated, angrier...hard to say. Mom set up a hidden camera that caught a vase fly across the room and...

(The sound of a shattering vase)

MELODY
That's what made my mom dive into the research. Turns out there's a lot of information out there if you're willing to look. And ninety percent of it is utter crap. Go back to the Seventies, Eighties...everyone was going nuts for the supernatural. From Stanford's research into ESP to Time Life's Mysteries of the Unknown, we had more than we knew what to do with. So you start sifting, searching for commonalities...and one of the big commonalities was electronic voice phenomenon. So we figured it was time to reach out and touch someone.

(They look at her)

MELODY
No, not...it's that old slogan. From AT&T.

(She sings the jingle)

MELODY
...reach out and touch...

(Beat)

MELODY
Anyway. We set the whole thing up. Got ourselves an EMF detector, so we'd know when the ghosts would be around. We got the recorder ready to go. So we waited. And waited and waited and waited and...

(The EMF detector goes off. MELODY joins MOM at the table)

MOM
They're here.

MELODY
Ok. Ok.

(MELODY addresses the audience)

MELODY
And so we asked our questions. It went on for over an hour, and we heard…nothing. Not at first. The next day, we played the recording back. This is what was on the tape.

(MOM faces the audience. The EVP is projected as a voiceprint. The sound of the ghost answers should be bizarre and echoed, ideally with subtitles making the response clear under the voiceprint)

MOM
Ok. Listen, these kids just want to know if you're here. Don't be mean or scary. We'll be cool if you will.

(No response)

MOM
Can you tell me your names?

(No response)

MOM
We've seen two of you here…the boy and the girl. Are there more spirits here?

(No response)

MOM
Are you brother and sister? Husband and wife?

(No response)

MOM
Did you live here? Did you...die here?

(No response)

MOM
Are you mad at us? Do you want us to leave?

(No response)

MOM
Are we doing something to anger you?

(No response. Beat. MOM sighs)

MOM
Can you tell us how you died?

EVP
NO!

MOM
Did you die a peaceful death, or a violent death?

EVP
NO NO NO NO NO NO NO NO

(The NOs repeat under the next several questions. They end in a wail)

MOM
Were you young when you died? Did you die in this house? In what room? Was it the garage? In the bedroom?

(The wail, then silence)

MOM
Why do you keep messing with us?

(No response)

MOM
Are we doing something you don't want us to do?

(No response)

MOM
Do you not want us in the garage?

(No response)

MOM
Do you not like it when Sam smokes in there?

(Two voices respond almost simultaneously, the male first and the female second)

EVP 1
No.

EVP 2
Well, you should know!

MOM
This is our house now. Do you understand that?

(No response)

MOM
You can share this place with us, or you can leave. Those are your two options.

(No response)

MOM
Is something holding you here? Why can't you move on?

EVP
Not that easy.

(MELODY addresses the audience)

MELODY
Mom went on for a while more, but that was the last thing they said to us. The weird stuff happened less after that, but it never stopped. Little things like getting your ear flicked, or finding the garbage can in the middle of the kitchen. But honestly, I think they did like us, that they'd gotten used to us. Because a few years later, we did move out of the house.

(MOM begins moving the items offstage)

MELODY
After we moved out, the new owner asked if we could give them the key to the garage because it was locked. There is no lock on the garage door. I think the spirits didn't want the new owner in their space. That girl probably. They were sad we were leaving. Sad...angry... whatever it was. I've thought about going back there a hundred times, asking the owners if they ever encountered anything. But I never have.

(AUTHOR addresses the audience)

AUTHOR
Sometimes you find answers. Sometimes you don't. But sometimes...you do.

(Projection: A window, with moonlight shining in)

AUTHOR
No.

TWO
If not now, when?

AUTHOR
When I'm ready.

FOUR
Isn't that why you're writing this? Because you're ready?

AUTHOR
I wanted to hear other stories. That's what I do! I collect stories!

THREE
So that you feel less alone, like you're not the only one who saw...?

AUTHOR
Weird shit happens all the time, ok? All the time! I don't need that confirmed!

TWO
It's just...we're at the end.

AUTHOR
Like hell we are!

(AUTHOR grabs a bunch of papers)

AUTHOR
There are so many stories, so many things people sent in! And my own research too! I had to winnow it down until...okay, here! Boneheads Barbecue.

(Beat)

AUTHOR
Boneheads freaking Barbecue!

(Projection: Boneheads Barbecue in Willis, MI)

AUTHOR
Willis, one of a hundred little Michigan towns that you'd maybe never find if you weren't looking for it. It's home to Boneheads Barbecue, and the skull logo they use has more than one meaning.

THREE
Come on.

AUTHOR
Quiet! I first found it eight years ago. Having spent several years living in the South, I'm always on the lookout for a good barbecue joint. Boneheads did not disappoint.

FOUR
You're evading.

AUTHOR
Part of the charm of Boneheads is the hauntings. Not one, not two, but THREE ghosts are supposed to keep the wait staff company there. The most frequent one is named Nellie. A woman in her forties, she's seen most frequently walking up and down the stairs in a flowing white dress.

(AUTHOR stares at the others, waiting for one of them to become NELLIE. No one moves)

TWO
It's time.

AUTHOR
The Ghost Hunters of Southeast Michigan conducted a thorough investigation, and determined that there are two other ghosts along with Nellie, all more mischievous than actually harmful.

(The others look at each other, then slowly exit the stage, leaving AUTHOR alone)

AUTHOR
The second is said to be a teenage girl who's fond of flickering lights and making chandeliers wave. She's also a sucker for appearing behind people when they look in the bathroom mirror.

(AUTHOR looks around, realizing the others are leaving)

AUTHOR
C'mon…the mirror thing…just…

(AUTHOR looks to audience)

AUTHOR
The restaurant even has a cat named Pickles who wanders about from time to time. The thing is, Pickles died years ago and is buried underneath the steps on the building's west side. So if you see something, feel something brush up against your leg…

(AUTHOR realizes that he is alone onstage)

AUTHOR
Don't leave me alone out here. Please.

(No response)

AUTHOR
Please.

(No response. AUTHOR sighs, rubs his face, then speaks to the audience)

AUTHOR
Something that stays with you, follows you, whether you want it to or not.

(Projection: An old house in Ypsilanti)

AUTHOR
I don't believe in ghosts. But I'm close. I'm damn close. Because I did see…something. Saw, heard, felt. But I don't know. I talked before about my night terrors. I've had dozens of them. This didn't feel like that. This felt… different.

(Beat)

AUTHOR
2002. Ypsilanti. We moved into a house in Ypsilanti. I told you this, I know.

(AUTHOR looks at the projection)

AUTHOR
This is the house. And you know what? I loved living there. It was comfortable. It was old. It was cheap. I was young. My roommate was my best friend from college. We both worked weird hours so we weren't around each other enough to get sick of. Mostly. Now, if he ever encountered anything in the house, he never said anything to me about it. I understand…because I never said anything to him about this either.

(Projection: A room at night. A single window, with moonlight streaming in. As AUTHOR speaks, the lights dim until only the projection can be seen)

AUTHOR
This would have been my second year living in the house. We'd already found the weird closet, I'd already had the nightmare about the robed people…yes, I'm still calling it a nightmare. And of course, the usual little things…floorboards creaking like someone's walking around, even when you're alone in the house. A cold breeze in the middle of a summer day. But I'm not the type who sees everyday crap and thinks, "GHOST!" If one version of a scenario can be explained rationally, and the other supernaturally, I'm going to go rational every single time, because…

(Beat)

AUTHOR

It makes you feel special, important, to encounter some-thing so bizarre. And let's be honest...lots of people do and say weird, weird stuff to feel important. They can even convince themselves that it's true. That's not me. I like the truth. I write fantasy, but I live reality. I think that's why this has stayed with me all this time...because explanations eluded me.

(A clock starts to chime. 3 AM)

AUTHOR

It was three in the morning. I know because I was awake. I woke right up and felt...weird. Back in the day, I could sleep through a Godzilla attack with a side of King Kong. But there I was, wide awake. I looked over and saw that ugly red digital clock reading 3:02. I was about to utter a colorful phrase but then I heard...it.

(The three remaining cast members have surreptitiously taken positions near or behind the audience. As one, they start to breathe heavily, growling as they do)

AUTHOR

The sound was right next to my ear. If there was something there, something physical, I would have felt its breath on my face. But I didn't feel anything. Not in the traditional sense of the word.

(Projection: The moonlight glows brighter)

AUTHOR

You've probably encountered it before...the feeling that you're not alone. That's what I felt, more so than the last dream...because I don't think this was a dream. I felt conscious, lucid. I froze solid at first, my mind think-ing there was some animal snarling in my ear. When I worked up the courage to look to my side...nothing there. I think that's what gave me the strength to sit up and look around the room. And what I saw…

(Projection: A ten-year-old child appears at the window, dressed in ragged 1800s clothing. The child is staring out the window)

AUTHOR
A kid. A little boy standing at the foot of my bed, dressed in rags. But he wasn't looking at me. He was staring out the window towards…I don't know. Something only he could see. I couldn't do anything at first. Not because I was paralyzed, because I was terrified. I was seeing this! My eyes were wide open and I was seeing this! Right in front of me! The room was freezing and I was drenched in sweat. It took every ounce of strength I had to just open my mouth. I tried to speak…I wanted to say, "Who are you?" but all I got out was "who…" when…

(Projection: The child turns, faces the audience)

AUTHOR
He turned and he looked right at me. Right at me. And suddenly, I was hit with this sensation, like a tidal wave. Sadness. Loss. Sorrow. Anger. And suddenly…

(Beat)

AUTHOR
It didn't speak in the way we think of speech. But it… communicated. Words or feelings, a single phrase hit me like a shotgun blast.

TWO/THREE/FOUR
You. Don't. Belong. Here.

AUTHOR
And just like that, I could move. The fight must have overcome the flight, and I jumped right out of my bed

and turned on the lights.

(The lights come up. The projection fades)

AUTHOR
Gone. Nothing there. Nothing I could see or feel, all in the time it takes to flip a light switch.

(AUTHOR takes a drink of water)

AUTHOR
Nightmare, or something more? I didn't know then anymore than I know now. I wish like hell I could definitively say it wasn't a night terror, that I'd seen a ghost right there in front of me. But this isn't one of those jackass ghost hunting documentaries, trying to squeeze out every possible drop of scary. This is…uncertainty.

(The other actors return to the stage)

AUTHOR
The event never left me. It haunted me. And I did what I love to do…I researched. I went to murders first. Murders that had happened on that street, ideally murders that had happened in that house.

(Beat)

AUTHOR
A few times a year, I'd go back on the hunt. But more than a decade later and still nothing.

(AUTHOR picks up a book on ghost-hunting)

AUTHOR
Was my own experience the impetus for the Great Lakes Ghost Project? Absolutely it was. My own research led me to other weird stories, so I cast a wide net and tried to see how many others I could catch. But it all led me back here.

(Projection: The old Ypsilanti house)

AUTHOR
While writing this, I reached back out to my old roommate. I asked him if he'd ever had any strange occur-
rences while we were living there. He said...

ROOMMATE
I remember a lot of creaking at night. Sometimes I
thought you were up walking around. The only scary
things were when you had a night terror. Second hand
night terrors, I guess.

AUTHOR
He was a good friend, and he'd seen me in the throws of
waking dreams many times.

ROOMMATE
Yeah, those were intense, coming out of a dead sleep to
the sound of someone being murdered, and then trying
to figure out in the dark just what the hell was going
on. Good times.

AUTHOR
They were not, in fact, good times.

ROOMMATE
I was always really impressed how well adjusted you
were, when your sleep was so terrifying.

AUTHOR
He asked me if I still had them, the dreams. I said no.
Luckily, for most of us that have them, they go away in
your mid-twenties. Fun fact: Night terrors only occur
in less than one percent of adults. Gotta love beating
the odds.

ROOMMATE
Your night terrors always seemed like an entity to me.

AUTHOR
An entity?

ROOMMATE
Yeah. Like something was attached to you, following us around to our various apartments. Or maybe you're just tuned in to that stuff. I don't know.

(Beat)

AUTHOR
God, I wish he hadn't put that thought in my mind.

ROOMMATE
Sorry.

AUTHOR
It had been a few years since I'd tried to dig up any information about our old place. As I was finishing the first draft of the Great Lakes Ghost Project, I said, "What the hell." I hopped online, doing all of my standard searches...street name, dates, murders...came up with the same amount of nothing. Once again, I made peace with the fact that answers are things that happen in stories, less so in real life. And then...I don't know...a whim, I guess. I'd always thought the kid was murdered because violent death, uneasy spirit, blahblahblah. But that was just a hunch. Hunches can be wrong. So instead of murder, I typed in the street name, 1800s, and death. What I found...turns out you can get answers in real life too.

(The projection fades)

AUTHOR
The cross street I used to live on had a different name back in the 1800s. That was why I kept coming up empty. It was called Chicago St. Once I connected the two

streets along with the basic years...holy shit.

(Projection. An old map of Chicago St. and Summit St. AUTHOR picks up a piece of paper and reads)

AUTHOR
From an old article found in the Ann Arbor Public Library.
"In the early part of the past century, Mrs. P.R. Cleary of Cleary College wondered why and how the children of the neighborhood were finding bones and bringing them home! They were finding them at the corner of Summit and Chicago St. Were they human or animal remains? Take them back and rebury them!

TWO
Even today, most have no knowledge of there being a cemetery at that location. Through the years, most of the land has been paved or housing erected on the site of the old cemetery.

THREE
Over the years, questions have been raised by researchers and neighbors over the cemetery. How many people were buried there? Were they moved, and if so what was done with the remains? Are there still remains at the location?

FOUR
Judge Larzelere gifted the original site to Ypsilanti in 1830. Charles Chapman in his 1881 book History of Washtenaw County: "West Cemetery was the first cemetery for the village of Ypsilanti. It was a crude burial place and was used from 1830-1847 and was said to be the resting place of 150-250 persons."

AUTHOR
As you read on, the writer discusses some controversy

over the cemetery until...

TWO
May 29, 1871: Summit Street Cemetery was "Declared vacated and abandoned for burial purposes...

THREE
...And notice is given to all persons with friends buried in Summit Cemetery that they have thirty days to move the bodies to their chosen location."

FOUR
According to a representative of Highland Cemetery...

AUTHOR
The new location.

FOUR
...the remains were removed by one man, one horse, one shovel, and one body at a time.

AUTHOR
The historical society was never able to find a registry of those who were formerly interred at Summit Street Cemetery, also known as West Cemetery. But yeah, the land was ploughed over, cemented, and built upon.

(AUTHOR motions to the map)

AUTHOR
This old map of the area still survives. Let's have a closer look, shall we?

(Projection: Tight image of the Old Cemetery location on the map, corner of Summit & Chicago)

AUTHOR
That block there, labeled Old Cemetery? That was the location of good old Summit Street Cemetery. Wanna take a guess where my old house was?

(AUTHOR points to the northernmost part of Old Cemetery)

AUTHOR
I lived there for three years, never knowing that I was sleeping not-so-soundly over a very, very old burial ground.

(The projection fades)

AUTHOR
Does this give me every single answer? No. I never learned the name of the child, and I doubt I ever will. I never saw a photo from that era that made me jump out of my chair and shout, "Him! That's him!" I'm still uncertain. I imagine I'll always be uncertain.

(A light centerstage, creating the sense of a campfire)

FOUR
A house is never still in darkness to those who listen intently.

THREE
There is a whispering in distant chambers, an unearthly hand presses the sill of the window, the latch rises.

TWO
Ghosts were created when the first man woke in the night.

AUTHOR
J.M. Barrie wrote that. Not a Midwesterner, true, but a good quote is a good quote.

(The actors all sit around the campfire)

AUTHOR
I didn't share these stories to tell you ghosts exist. I don't know if they do, and I don't know if they don't.

TWO
The things that creep in the night...maybe they're just campfire stories. They scare, but they thrill too.

FOUR
Maybe. Or maybe those moments when you feel like there's something there, something you can't quite see... you might not be as alone as you think.

(The lights begin to dim very slowly until the cast is lit only by the campfire)

THREE
So we light fires, to chase away the shadows. And hopefully the things hiding in those shadows.

ONE
It's October. And the Great Lakes do October very, very well.

FOUR
We celebrate the harvest with cider and hayrides.

TWO
Corn mazes and horror movies.

ONE
Masks and costumes and trick-or-treating.

FOUR
And we gather around our bonfires, huddled close for warmth.

TWO
Maybe there's s'mores.

THREE
Maybe there's music.

(They warm their hands around the fire)

ONE
It's October in the Midwest, and there's nothing else like it. It has a magic all its own. You can smell it in the air and hear it in the wind. We celebrate it in a million different ways, but when we gather around the fire...

TWO
I was eighteen when I saw it.

FOUR
I was twelve...

THREE
Ten...

ONE
...twenty-five when I saw it.

TWO
Just a girl.

FOUR
No bigger than this.

ONE
...there are always ghost stories.

(Lights fade as the campfire goes out)

END OF PLAY

ABOUT THE PLAYWRIGHT

Joseph Zettelmaier is a Michigan-based playwright and four-time nominee for the Steinberg/American Theatre Critics Association Award for best new play, first in 2006 for ALL CHILDISH THINGS, then in 2007 for LANGUAGE LESSONS, in 2010 for IT CAME FROM MARS and in 2012 for ALL CHILDISH THINGS. Other plays include SALVAGE, THE GRAVEDIGGER - A FRANKENSTEIN PLAY, NORTHERN AGGRESSION, DR. SEWARD'S DRACULA, INVASIVE SPECIES, THE SCULLERY MAID, NIGHT BLOOMING, and EBENEZER.

POINT OF ORIGIN won Best Locally Created Script 2002 from the Ann Arbor News, and THE STILLNESS BETWEEN BREATHS also won Best New Play 2005 from the Oakland Press. THE STILLNESS BETWEEN BREATHS and IT CAME FROM MARS were selected to appear in the National New Play Network's Festival of New Plays. He also co-authored Flyover, USA: Voices From Men of the Midwest at the Williamston Theatre (Winner of the 2009 Thespie Award for Best New Script). He also adapted CHRISTMAS CAROL'D for the Performance Network.

IT CAME FROM MARS was a recipient of 2009's Edgerton Foundation New American Play Award, and won Best New Script 2010 from the Lansing State Journal. His play ALL CHILDISH THINGS won the Edgerton Foundation New American Play Award in 2011.

Joseph is a founding member of the Roustabout Theatre Company and an Associate Artist at First Folio Shakespeare, an Artistic Ambassador to the National New Play Network, and an adjunct lecturer at Eastern Michigan University, where he teaches Dramatic Composition.

MORE FROM SORDELET INK
PLAYSCRIPTS

WWW.SORDELETINK.COM

SORDELET INK NOVELS BY DAVID BLIXT

NELLIE BLY
WHAT GIRLS ARE GOOD FOR
CHARITY GIRL
CLEVER GIRL

THE STAR-CROSS'D SERIES
THE MASTER OF VERONA
VOICE OF THE FALCONER
FORTUNE'S FOOL
THE PRINCE'S DOOM
VARNISH'D FACES: STAR-CROSS'D SHORT STORIES

WILL & KIT
HER MAJESTY'S WILL

THE COLOSSUS SERIES
COLOSSUS: STONE & STEEL
COLOSSUS: THE FOUR EMPERORS

EVE OF IDES—A PLAY

NON-FICTION
SHAKESPEARE'S SECRETS: ROMEO & JULIET
TOMORROW, AND TOMORROW: ESSAYS ON MACBETH
FIGHTING WORDS

THE MYSTERY OF CENTRAL PARK

A rejected marriage proposal and the corpse of a dead beauty confound Dick Treadwell's hopes for happiness, until his beloved Penelope sets him a task: she will marry him if he solves— *the Mystery of Central Park!*

EVA, THE ADVENTURESS

Nellie Bly's ripped-from-the-headlines novel of a poor girl determined to revenge herself upon the world, only to find that, in the battle between love and revenge, only one can triumph.

NEW YORK BY NIGHT

Setting out to solve the bold diamond robbery, millionaire detective Lionel Dangerfield finds himself in competition with Ruby Sharpe, daring young reporter for the *New York Planet*. Will "The Danger" solve the case before Ruby can steal the story—and his heart?

ALTA LYNN, M.D.

A prank goes awry and Alta Lynn finds herself wed against her will. Leaving love behind, she throws herself into the study of medicine, only to find that love has other plans for her!

WAYNE'S FAITHFUL SWEETHEART

Beautiful Dorette Lover is rescued from poverty when she finds work as an artist's model. That same day she witnesses a seeming murder. To protect the man accused, she agrees to become his bride—only to fall desperately in love with him!

LITTLE LUCKIE

Luckie Thurlow longs to be accepted by society and gain the man she loves. But she harbors a dark secret—she is the daughter of the murderous Gypsy Queen, who plans to use Luckie to gain her own revenge!

IN LOVE WITH A STRANGER

Kit Clarendon is in love! Trouble is, she doesn't know her love's name. But she is determined to track him down and force him to love her! A wild pursuit filled with disguises, desperate deeds, and declarations of love as Kit determines to go through fire and water to win him!

THE LOVE OF THREE GIRLS

An heiress in disguise, a factory girl with dreams of wealth, and a sweet child of charity are forced into rivalry when they all fall in love with the same man! Murder, fever, fallen women, and a desperate villain conspire against— *the love of three girls!*

INTO THE MADHOUSE

Never before collected! "Who is this insane girl?" asked other papers, completely taken in by Nellie Bly's plan to infiltrate Blackwell's Island. The complete reporting surrounding her daring expose, including details not included in her initial accounts and her scathing rebuttal of the doctors' excuses!

NELLIE BLY'S WORLD—Vol. 1
1887-1888

Bly's complete reporting, collected for the very first time! Starting with the stunt that made hers a household name, Nellie Bly spends her first year at the New York World going undercover to expose frauds, sharpsters and boodlers, interviewing Belva Lockwood and Hangman Joe, and tackling Phelps the Lobbyist!

NELLIE BLY'S WORLD—Vol. 2
1889-1890

Bly's complete reporting, collected for the very first time! Nellie buys a baby, has herself followed by a detective and arrested, interviews Helen Keller, champion boxer John Sullivan, and convicted would-be killer Eva Hamilton, all before setting out on her greatest stunt of all, a race around the world!

COMING SOON:

NELLIE BLY'S WORLD, Vol. 3 & 4
NELLIE BLY'S DISPATCHES, Vol. 1 & 2
NELLIE BLY's JOURNALS, Vol. 1 & 2

ALL FROM SORDELET INK